Book 1

All That Glitters

JILL SANTOPOLO

Aladdin

NEW YORK LONDON TORONTO SYDNEY NEW DELHI

ALADDIN

An imprint of Simon & Schuster Children's Publishing Division

1230 Avenue of the Americas, New York, NY 10020

This Aladdin paperback edition July 2017

Text copyright © 2014 by Simon & Schuster, Inc.

Cover illustrations and interior spot illustrations copyright © 2014 by Cathi Mingus

Book design by Jeanine Henderson

All rights reserved, including the right of reproduction in whole or in part in any form.

ALADDIN and related logo are registered trademarks of Simon & Schuster, Inc.

Also available in an Aladdin hardcover edition.

For information about special discounts for bulk purchases, please contact Simon & Schuster Special Sales at 1-866-506-1949 or business@simonandschuster.com.

The Simon & Schuster Speakers Bureau can bring authors to your live event. For more information or to book an event, contact the Simon & Schuster Speakers Bureau at 1-866-248-3049 or visit our website at www.simonspeakers.com.

The text of this book was set in Adobe Caslon.

Manufactured in the United States of America 0717 OFF

10 9 8 7 6 5 4 3 2 1

Library of Congress Control Number 2013949501

ISBN 978-1-4424-7381-2 (hc)

ISBN 978-1-4424-7380-5 (pbk)

ISBN 978-1-4424-7382-9 (eBook)

ISBN 978-1-5344-1300-9 (proprietary pbk)

For my niece, Lily Paige May.

May your life be filled with love, happiness,

and more than a little bit of sparkle.

Special glittery thanks to Karen Nagel,

editrix extraordinaire, as well as to Marianna Baer,

Betsy Bird, Jessica Ann Carp, Andrea Cremer,

Kekla Magoon, Marie Rutkoski, and Eliot Schrefer,

all writers who glimmer and glow.

Contents

one

Under Watermelon

The school bell rang, and Aly raced out the door, holding on tight to her backpack straps.

"Slow down!" a hall monitor shouted after her, but Aly didn't listen. She made it to the steps at the front of the school in record time.

Her purple polka-dot watch said 3:07. Only eight minutes until Arnold the deliveryman arrived at her mom's nail salon. Aly *really* wanted to be there to meet him. All the new sparkle colors were supposed to come that day, and Mom had promised that Aly and her sister, Brooke, could test them out the minute they arrived.

Where *was* Brooke? It took exactly five minutes to walk to the nail salon, which was three and a half blocks from Auden Elementary. Now Aly's watch said 3:08. That meant they'd have two minutes to spare, if Brooke came right away.

Aly turned around, looking through the doorway into the school. When she squinted, she was pretty certain she saw Brooke, her long, braided ponytail swinging back and forth, skipping down the hall with three other third graders. This was not the time for skipping!

"Brooke!" Aly yelled.

Brooke looked up, broke away from the other skipping girls, and ran toward Aly. When she got to the door, she was out of breath. "The sparkles! I almost forgot!" she said. "They must've skipped right out of my head!"

Aly loved her sister a lot, but Brooke was not the best at remembering. She was good at a lot of things, like (1) being a nail polish tester and (2) guessing which colors would be popular. But Aly was better at remembering. She was also better at making lists. Lots of lists. They helped keep all her thoughts organized. Brooke's thoughts were hardly ever organized.

"How many minutes do we have?" Brooke asked, pushing her glasses up to the top of her nose.

Aly looked at her watch again. "Six!" she said. "Time for racewalking!"

The two girls took off, walking their fastest, pumping their arms back and forth to get extra speed. There was a man in their town who was an expert racewalker and always wore pink shorts and a pink T-shirt the exact color of Ready Set Flamingo nail polish. Aly and Brooke called him Mr. Flamingo and liked to walk the speedy way he did when they were in a hurry. Elbows were involved.

"Aly, did we end up ordering Cherry, Cherry Nice?" Brooke asked, panting a little as they race-walked past the pet store and the empty shop across from the salon that used to be the Candy Bar.

Aly knew all the colors by heart. She'd helped Mom put in the order. "No Cherry, Cherry Nice," she said. "We got Strawberry Sunday, Under Watermelon, Lemon Aid, Orange You Pretty, and We the Purple."

Brooke thought for a second. "I bet Lemon Aid will be the most popular."

"Lemon Aid?" Aly asked. True Colors was only a few doors down now. Aly could see the sign—light blue with pink and purple curlicue letters. It was 3:14. One minute until Arnold!

"Yes," Brooke said. "Lemon Aid. Yellow hasn't been popular before. It needs a turn."

Now that she was a fifth grader, Aly knew that just

because you hadn't been popular before didn't mean you'd ever get a turn. Suzy Davis, who was the meanest girl in her whole grade, had never been popular. She'd just been mean. Ever since kindergarten. But then again, yellow was a color, and colors couldn't be mean, so maybe it was different with nail polish.

The sisters reached the front door of True Colors at the exact same time Arnold did. He was holding a big box in his arms.

"Hi, Arnold! Are the sparkles here?" Brooke asked. She was tugging on her braid, which she always did when she was extra excited. Or extra nervous. This time, the pulling was definitely for excitement.

"Right here!" he said, bending over so Brooke could see the package. "Aly, can you sign for it, please?"

Aly nodded. It was a job her mom had given her last year, once she was able to write her name perfectly in script.

Arnold gave Aly his signing machine and a plastic thing that looked like a pen. She signed *Alyssa Tanner* on the screen in her most careful handwriting. Then he took back his machine and handed her the box.

Brooke jumped up and down. "Can I hold it, Aly? Pleeeaassee!" she begged.

"You know the rules," Aly said. "Carrying boxes of nail polish is a fifth-grade-and-older job."

Brooke picked up her backpack, which was covered in twirly pictures she'd drawn on with old nail polish colors. "I know. But it was worth a try," she said as she held the door open for her sister.

Door opening was a third-grade job. Actually, it was a first-grade job, but it was one you could keep doing until you graduated from elementary school and turned a million years old. In the nail salon there were a lot of rules about what you could and couldn't do based on how old you were.

The bells on top of the door jingled as it closed behind Aly. Everyone in the salon turned to look. The place was packed—even the six waiting-for-a-manicure chairs near the front window were filled.

"Hi, girls!" a few of the manicurists said.

"I have cookies for you two," said Joan, who was Aly and Brooke's favorite manicurist. "Raisin chocolate chip." Joan wanted to open her own bakery one day.

"Hi, sweeties," their mom said, looking up from manicure station number one. She carefully squeezed a rhinestone with a pair of tweezers, about to glue it on Miss Nina's left pinkie nail. Miss Nina was one of the dog groomers at the pet store down the street and was a True Colors regular. She loved getting rhinestones on her pinkies.

"We got the new sparkles," Brooke announced as she raced toward a room at the back of the salon.

"I signed for the package," Aly added. She passed

the row of five huge teal pedicure chairs—all filled—
and walked around the ten manicure stations. Joan's
was number seven. All those stations were filled too.

"That's great!" their mom called after them. "Pretzels
and juice are in the back. And if you're still hungry after
that, you can each have one of Joan's cookies."

"Whoo-hoo!" Brooke yelled.

The bell jingled again, and more people walked
in. Aly couldn't believe how busy the salon was.

While Aly and Brooke munched on their pretzels—
and Joan's cookies—Brooke decided she wanted rainbow sparkle toes. One new color on each toe, starting
with Strawberry Sunday on her big toe, followed by
Orange You Pretty, Lemon Aid, We the Purple, and,
on her baby toe, Under Watermelon.

It wasn't a regular rainbow, because there was no
blue or green and it ended in pink, but Aly could see how
it might look cool. Still, she wanted to double-check.

It was always good to double-check, just in ... ple changed their minds. Especially when th ... fast decisions, like Brooke.

"Are you positively sure?" Aly ask ... never new colors arrived, Aly was usually th ... painter and Brooke was usually the tester. It wor ... ed well that way because Aly was a very careful painter and Brooke picked good combinations to try.

"Certain," Brooke answered. She left her napkin and cup on the table and ran over to one of the old pedicure chairs in the corner. The blue-green leather on the chairs was worn out in some places, so Mom had them moved to the back. Brooke hopped into the chair on the right and slipped off her sandals, and Aly got started.

Aly had been practicing her polishing skills since she was in kindergarten. Brooke had been practicing too, but Aly was the expert. Aly had taught Brooke:

- Keep the side of your hand resting on something steady for wobble-free polishing.
- Wipe extra polish off on the side of the bottle before you paint a nail.
- People's feet are very ticklish.
- Red polish stains white shorts.
- So does purple.

And Brooke had taught herself how to stay super still while she was getting her toes painted—even if Aly tickled her or dripped polish on her shorts.

One by one, Aly applied the glittery colors. "They look so beautiful," Brooke whispered. "I love the sparkles. They are so . . . so . . ."

"Sparkly?" Aly said, and they both started laughing.

Aly tucked her hair behind her ears. It had been cut too short to pull into a ponytail, perhaps not the best hairstyle for a manicurist. She kept worrying that it would fall in front of her eyes and that she'd paint Brooke's skin instead of her nails. Maybe she should ask Mom to buy her some headbands.

After she'd applied a second coat, Aly admired Brooke's toes herself. She had to admit, the rainbow look was awesome, especially with the sparkles.

"Let's go see if there's a spot at the drying station, Brookester."

Brooke stood up and hobbled on her heels, following Aly out of the back room and into the main salon.

"I am the Princess of Sparkles," Brooke announced. Brooke would say or do anything, Aly thought, to make people pay attention to her. Mostly Aly didn't mind, but sometimes it could get annoying.

"Come over here and show me your royal toes," Mom said. She was by the door, helping Miss Nina get her car keys out of her bag so she wouldn't smudge her new manicure.

"Nice color choices, Brookie. And nice job, Aly."

"Maybe you could do my nails next week." Miss Nina winked at Aly. "You're just as good as your mom."

Aly smiled as Miss Nina left the salon. She was *so* ready to be a real manicurist, but Mom said she had to wait until she was eighteen. School had to be her main job until then. After that, she could paint nails. Or go to college. Or do both. Aly wasn't sure what she would choose.

"Do you like the rainbow?" Aly asked.

"Very much," said Mom.

"What rainbow?"

Aly looked up. Sitting on one of the chairs in the waiting area was Jenica Posner. *The* Jenica Posner—a sixth grader who was the very best soccer player on the girls' team.

And this was the first time she had ever spoken to Aly.

two

Strawberry Sunday

Aly couldn't answer. Her mouth opened, but no words came out. She just stared at Jenica. But Brooke chattered away like Jenica was her very best friend.

"There's a rainbow of sparkle polish on my toes," Brooke told her. Brooke wasn't shy around anyone. Not even sixth graders. Not even Jenica Posner.

Jenica got up and walked across the nail salon. "These are totally cool!" She kneeled down and inspected Brooke's toes.

"Can I get mine done like that, Nana?" she asked. Jenica turned her head toward a woman with a long white ponytail sitting at station number two.

"If they have time for you, honey. You'll have to ask," the woman answered.

Aly and Brooke's mom flipped through the pages of the salon's appointment book. She looked at the people in the waiting area. There were now more people waiting than there were chairs for them to sit on.

"I'm so sorry, sweetie," she said to Jenica, "but we're all booked up. Maybe tomorrow?"

"Tomorrow I have a soccer game," Jenica said. "Too bad."

Brooke looked at Aly. She winked once with her left eye, then twice with her right, trying to send a Secret Sister Eye Message. But Aly was having trouble understanding it. Finally, Brooke blurted out, "Aly, Mom! Aly could do it!"

Aly felt a rush of excitement. But she knew the rules. Brooke must have forgotten. "I can't," Aly whispered to her sister. "Not till I'm eighteen."

But Jenica didn't hear Aly's whispers. "Could she?" Jenica asked Aly's mom.

Aly held her breath. What would Mom say?

"Well . . ." Mom looked at the crowded shop and then at Aly. "Maybe just this once. As long as it's okay with you, Aly. Same rules as when you do Brooke's nails—no clippers, no cuticle cutters, just emery boards and polish."

"It's okay with me," Aly said as calmly as she could. But her stomach was flipping around like it was doing somersaults off a diving board.

"This one's on the house," Aly heard her mom say to Jenica's nana.

Since all the pedicure chairs were full, Aly and Brooke took Jenica to the back room.

"Brooke, please turn on the water at pedicure station one," Aly said, pretending that she and Brooke gave pedicures every day. "Jenica, sit over there, please."

"Okay, but which is station one?" Brooke asked.

Aly rolled her eyes. "You know . . . the left one."

Brooke turned on the faucet, and as the basin filled with water, Aly removed Jenica's old—and very chipped—toenail polish.

"Soccer's rough on toenail polish," Jenica said, flexing her big toes.

"I know what you mean," Aly answered, even though she really didn't. Weren't Jenica's toes protected by cleats while she played soccer?

"I think the water's ready!" Brooke chirped, slipping under Aly's arm to turn off the faucet. "Do you play soccer a lot? What about other sports? Do you play them, too?"

"Just soccer," Jenica said to Brooke. "Do I put my feet in now?"

Aly nodded as she added a drop of special skin-softening oil to the water. "It should be nice and warm and feel—"

"YIKES!" Jenica yelled. She yanked her feet out of the water. "That's *freezing*! I can't put my feet in there!"

Aly dipped her hand in the water. It felt like the tub of melted ice that her dad stored drinks in at barbecues.

"Brooke! Did you adjust the temperature?"

Brooke shrugged. "I thought I did. Sorry!"

Didn't Brooke understand that this was Jenica Posner? And that they couldn't mess up her pedicure?

Aly let the water drain, adjusted the temperature, and refilled the basin.

Finally, when Jenica's feet were clean and dry—and warm!—Aly gripped the bottom of her foot, just like she held Brooke's when she painted her toenails. But Jenica apparently hadn't practiced sitting still the way Brooke had.

She started laughing. "I'm really ticklish!" she said. "You can't touch my foot like that!"

Aly took a deep breath. She wasn't sure how to fix this, and if Jenica kept laughing, there was no way this pedicure could ever happen. Even though she was still sort of annoyed at Brooke about the cold water, Aly looked at her sister and opened her eyes as wide as possible. Code for *Help!*

"I know how you can stop feeling tickly," Brooke said to Jenica. "It's the trick I use when Aly paints my nails." She paused for a second. "Bite on your tongue. Not so hard that it bleeds or anything, but just so you feel it. Then you think about your tongue and you don't think about your feet being ticklish. And the tickle feeling goes away. Like magic."

Brooke smiled. "I came up with that myself."

Jenica looked horrified. "You want me to bite my tongue?"

"Not *hard*," Brooke said. "Just a little bit. I promise it works."

Jenica looked at Aly. Aly shrugged. "She never laughs when I polish her toes."

"This is weird," Jenica said. "But I'll try it."

Jenica bit down on her tongue, and slowly and carefully, Aly lifted Jenica's foot and started painting her toes with two coats of rainbow-colored sparkles.

After two toes were done, Jenica said, "You're right, Brooke. It works—it doesn't tickle anymore." She held out her hand, and Brooke high-fived it.

Aly was just thankful that the trick had worked as she concentrated on the job in front of her. She'd gotten two more nails done when her hair slipped in front of her right eye. Dumb haircut.

"Did you just get that red on my actual toe?" Jenica asked, wiggling her foot.

Aly rested the polish brush on the floor and tucked her hair back behind her ear. Then she looked down. Oops!

"Sorry about that," she said. She grabbed a little wooden stick, dipped it in polish remover, and wiped the polish off Jenica's toe. "I think I need a headband to keep my hair back."

"You totally do," Brooke said. Then she turned to Jenica. "She totally does."

Jenica pulled an elastic out of her own hair and handed it to Aly. "Why don't you do a half-up with this? It'll keep it out of your eyes."

Jenica Posner, the superstar sixth-grade soccer player, was giving Aly an elastic right off her own head? Aly couldn't believe it, but she did what Jenica said, putting half of her hair up on top of her head.

Then she took a deep breath and kept painting. This was more nerve-wracking than being in the district-wide spelling bee, and that had been one of the most nerve-wracking days of Aly's life!

"You're actually good at this," Jenica said as, stroke by stroke, Aly transformed Jenica's toes into a sparkly rainbow. No more polish got on Jenica's skin. Not even a drop. And thanks to Brooke's tongue trick, Jenica didn't laugh or wriggle anymore.

"Aly's not just regular good," Brooke said, "she's especially, fabulously good. She polishes my nails all the time. And sometimes, at home, she polishes my cousins' nails, and once my grandma's, and when we were little, she polished our stuffed animals' nails, but she got in trouble for that."

Aly cringed. Why oh why did Brooke have to tell Jenica about the stuffed animals?

Jenica laughed. "I bet your mom wasn't too happy with that one."

"Nope, not at all. For her punishment—"

"Brooke, do we have clear polish back here?" Aly asked. She knew they did, but she *had* to do something to get Brooke to stop telling Jenica Posner such embarrassing things about her.

Brooke got the clear polish. Then she started talking about Arnold and how he delivered all the polish to True Colors.

Feeling much calmer, Aly added a clear coat on top of the colors—something she didn't do for Brooke. It was what the real manicurists did, though.

"All done!" Aly said, and smiled.

Jenica lifted her feet out in front of her. "I can't wait to show the girls on the soccer team. They're going to flip."

"Well, if you tell them to call for appointments,

my mom can schedule them for rainbow sparkle pedicures too," Aly said as she opened the basin's drain.

"Good idea," Jenica said, standing up. "Can I walk?"

"Really carefully," Aly told her. "Mostly on your heels. To the toe-drying station out front. Brooke, can you bring Jenica's flip-flops, please?"

After Jenica's polish was dry, she said to Aly, "I'm going to tell the team to ask for you. This is the prettiest pedicure I've ever had."

Aly couldn't stop a huge smile from spreading across her face. Out of all of the days she'd spent at True Colors—even with Jenica almost freezing her feet off, and Brooke's humiliating stories, and Strawberry Sunday just about sticking Jenica's toes together—Aly was pretty sure this was the best one yet.

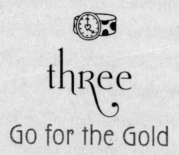

thREE

Go for the Gold

The next morning Aly, Brooke, and two Pop-Tarts— chocolate for Aly and strawberry for Brooke—were in the backseat of their mom's car. It was so early that Brooke had finished braiding only one side of her hair. The other side hung down almost to her waist.

True Colors was opening an hour earlier than usual. One of the Saturday regulars, Miss Lulu, was getting married in the afternoon. Twelve bridesmaids were coming with her to the salon for matching Just Peachy manicures and pedicures.

After Miss Lulu and her wedding party left, a birthday girl was scheduled to come in with her two sisters and three friends before her Sweet Sixteen party. This was all in addition to the Saturday regulars and whoever else called for an appointment.

"Stop wriggling, Brooke. This side is totally crooked. It looks like it's coming out of your ear," Aly said with a giggle, trying to braid Brooke's hair while holding her Pop-Tart between her knees.

"Please, girls, keep it down back there," Mom said, glancing in the rearview mirror. "I can barely keep my thoughts straight. There's so much to get done today. And Dad won't be home until tomorrow."

Aly looked at her watch: 7:50. Mom seemed exhausted already. Dad was supposed to have been home from his business trip by now, but his flight last night was canceled at the last minute.

At the next red light Mom twisted around to look

at the girls. "Brooke," she said, "you have an important job today."

Through a mouthful of Pop-Tart, Brooke mumbled, "I do?"

"It's going to be a busy Saturday. You know what that means: bottles of polish all over the salon. Can you keep an eye on the colors and make sure there aren't any purples in the red section or blues in the orange section—that kind of thing?"

"Sure, Mom," she answered. "That's easy."

Organizing polish colors was one of Brooke's favorite jobs—and the one she was best at. The colors would go slowly from red to orange to gold to yellow to green to blue to purple to silver to black to brown. When she was done, the arrangement would look like it belonged in an art museum. Brooke did the same thing to her crayons and to the clothes hanging in her closet. She even did it to the books on her bookshelves.

When the red light turned green, Aly asked, "What can I do to help?"

Usually, she had a bunch of small jobs:

- Making sure the manicurists had enough hot towels
- Signing for packages
- Playing with toddlers
- Emptying trash cans
- Sweeping the floor
- Helping customers with their car keys and purses
- Running over to the bank to trade a few twenty-dollar bills for a ton of one-dollar bills

"I need you to answer the phone and make appointments in the schedule book," Mom said, pulling the car into the parking lot behind the salon.

Aly couldn't believe it. She'd never done that before.

She'd figured that was a high school job for sure. Or eighth grade at least.

"Do you mean it, Mom?" she asked.

The three got out of the car and walked to the rear entrance together. "Let's see how it goes until we're done with Lulu's wedding. Then I'll take over. But I'm sure you'll do fine," Mom said, opening the door.

"No problem. I'll do my best," Aly told her mom. Aly thought Brooke would be a *much* better phone answerer because she never, ever stopped talking. Well, except when she was eating a Pop-Tart.

At 8:00 a.m. on the dot, Joan unlocked the front door to True Colors. In rushed Miss Lulu and her Just Peachy bridesmaids. They filled up all five pedicure chairs plus manicure stations one through eight.

First Brooke did her usual job of offering people

cups of water. Then she positioned herself right next to the polish display.

Aly was already seated at the front desk with the telephone and the appointment book. She felt kind of silly just sitting there, looking around at the yellow walls and stacks of magazines, doing nothing except listening to Brooke ask Miss Lulu a gazillion questions about her wedding.

"What color are your shoes?"

"Is your veil long?"

"Do you like roses?"

"Is your wedding cake chocolate? That's my favorite flavor."

Aly opened the appointment book. It was pretty full already, but there were a few slots open for pedicures in the afternoon and even more for manicures.

The first time the phone rang, Aly froze. Brooke

raced over and poked her arm. "Aly! Pick up the phone!"

Aly swallowed hard. On the third ring she answered. "True Colors. May I help you?"

On the other end, a girl asked for a rainbow sparkle pedicure at two o'clock. "My friend Jenica got one yesterday. And, oh, and, um, can Aly do it?" she asked.

Aly wanted to say yes, but she knew the rules. She had to be eighteen. And there were still open spots for the regular manicurists, which had to get filled.

"Aly can't do it," Aly said, pretending she was someone else. "But we can fit you in at two twenty. Will that work?"

"I can come then. Are you sure Aly can't do it?"

Aly swallowed again. "I'm sure," she said. "What's your name?"

"Bethany," the girl answered.

"Okay, thanks, Bethany. We'll see you later," Aly said, and hung up.

She wanted to tell Mom about Bethany asking for her. But Mom was in the middle of painting Miss Lulu's nails—a French manicure, pink on the bottom with white tips, and a rhinestone on her wedding ring finger—and needed to concentrate.

The phone rang again: two mani appointments for a woman and her husband. Then it rang a third time: another one of Jenica's friends, Mia, also asking for a rainbow sparkle pedicure. From Aly. The phone kept ringing and ringing until almost all the empty spots were booked.

Just as it started to calm down, a few walk-ins arrived. As Aly was taking down their names on the waiting list, her mom came over.

"Thanks, sweetie," she said. "I'll take it from here. Your sister's in the back room with some lemonade."

Aly stood up. "We're all booked up for pedicures," she told her mom. "Oh, and two people called about getting the same rainbow sparkle pedicure I gave Brooke and Jenica yesterday."

"We're *all* booked up for pedicures?" her mother asked. "Already?"

Mom ran her fingers through her hair. Aly spotted Just Peachy polish splotched on her elbow.

"I hate turning customers away," Mom said. "This is great, but . . ."

Aly didn't like it when her mom frowned. "Maybe no one else will want a pedicure today," she offered.

"Maybe," Mom said, but she didn't seem like she really believed it.

On her way to the back room Aly straightened the frames of the flower pictures on the walls and stopped to say hi to Mrs. Franklin, one of her favorite regulars. She had a tiny dog named Sadie. Sadie was a professional dog model. Mrs. Franklin carried around pictures of her dressed in different costumes from her photo shoots. Aly especially liked the one of Sadie dressed in a tutu with a bright pink flower in her collar. It was for some sort of dog food commercial.

Once Aly was inside, Brooke handed her a cup of lemonade.

"It's crazy out there!" Brooke said. "We need more paper cups. We ran out of Raspberry Good. And Miss Lulu hates roses!" Both girls flopped into the pedicure chairs.

"Crazy is right," Aly said, enjoying the sweet-and-sour taste the lemonade left on her tongue. "The appointment book is almost filled too."

Brooke waited for Aly to finish her drink. "So," she said, "since it's Saturday . . ." She pulled a bottle of gold glitter polish out of her shorts pocket. Go for the Gold. It was from a shipment two weeks ago.

Aly took the bottle. She'd almost forgotten! It was like they were in a backward world, where Brooke remembered things and Aly didn't!

The girls were always allowed to wear *toe* polish, but they had permission to wear *nail* polish only on weekends. So every Saturday they painted each other's nails. Well, Aly painted both of Brooke's hands and one of her own. Then Brooke did Aly's other hand, even though her polishing was a little wobbly. There was no other choice, because Aly's left hand wasn't as good at polishing as her right hand was.

"Let's get started," Aly said.

She painted Brooke's fingers, then the fingers on her own left hand. While she polished, Brooke peeked into the main salon.

"No way are there open dryers out there," Brooke said. "We'll have to fan." She started waving her hands around so the air would speed up the drying.

Just as Aly was finishing up her left pinkie and about to give the polish brush to Brooke, their mother came in. Now she had a splotch of Plum Delicious on her chin!

"This has to be the busiest Saturday we've ever had. I'll need you both out front when you're done with your break," she said.

"Look!" Brooke said, wiggling her glimmering gold-tipped fingers.

"Beautiful!" Mom answered, and then she caught one of Brooke's hands in her own. "And great manicure, Aly. Oh, by the way, three more of your friends called for a rainbow sparkle pedicure. I had to tell them we were booked for today. They asked for you too. I guess you made a real impression."

The idea of people calling and asking for her made Aly a little breathless. "Too bad I'm not eighteen yet," she said. "Then I could've done their pedicures."

"Mom, why does Aly have to wait?" Brooke asked. "I *hate* that rule! She's so good."

Mom inspected Brooke's fingers a little more closely and gave Aly a funny look. But then Carla appeared at the door. "Your eleven o'clock is here, Karen."

Mom let go of Brooke's hand. "Thanks," she said. "I've got to get back to it, girls."

When Mom left, Brooke finished painting Aly's nails. Aly was surprised by how nice it looked.

"You're going to be just as good as me soon," Aly told her sister.

And somehow, saying that made an idea explode in Aly's brain.

"Brooke . . . what if we ask Mom about opening our own salon, here in the back room, just for kids? I know we're not eighteen, but she *did* let me polish Jenica's toes. So maybe if there's one exception, there could be more!"

As the words came out of her mouth, Aly couldn't tell if they were really smart or really silly. "We're both pretty good manicurists, and Mom wouldn't have to turn down customers who want rainbow sparkle pedicures!"

Brooke started tugging on her left braid like she might pull it out of her head. "Really?" she asked. "Do you really, *really* think we could?"

"I think so," Aly said. "But it'll probably take some convincing."

Brooke looked thoughtful. "What kind of convincing?" she asked.

"Well," Aly said, "first we'd probably need to write up a plan and give it to Mom. That way, she'll take us seriously, like she does when people come by selling nail dryers and clippers and stuff. They give her lots of papers with information on them."

Brooke pushed her glasses up, tight against her

face. "Okay. We can come up with a plan. But right now I need to neaten up the polish shelves. And I promised Mrs. Franklin I'd look at Sadie's new pictures. Also, Joan asked me to refill her box of rhinestones because she's running low."

Aly nodded. "Let's meet back here when Mom gives us another break," she said. But she had already started making a list in her head.

And as she did, she had the feeling that this was not just a good idea, but an awesome one. At least she hoped it was.

Aly just had to figure out how to make Mom break her own rules so it could happen.

four

Green with Envy

True Colors Problems

1. Too crowded
2. Customers don't like waiting
3. Lots of kids want pedicures (not a
   problem, just a fact)

How OUR Salon Could Fix the Problems

1. Two more polishers, so more nails can
   get done
2. More spots for grown-ups in the main salon

Brooke read the list over Aly's shoulder, moving her mouth with the words. When she was finished, she clapped her hands. "That's perfect," she said. "But I have more to add."

Aly scribbled a little bit to get the ink flowing again, then said, "Go for it. What else?"

"Well," Brooke said, "we can experiment on the other kids to see how new colors look, so I don't have to be the only tester. And we can host polish parties, like the one for the Sweet Sixteen girl today, but for younger kids. And we could polish little kids' nails while their moms are getting manicures—kind of like babysitting—so they don't get bored from waiting."

Aly wrote very quickly. When she finished, she put down her pen. "Those are great ideas, Brooke. You should be a professional idea person."

Brooke smiled. "That would be a fun job. Except

I think I might want to be an organizer instead. And also a manicurist. And an artist."

Aly thought Brooke would be good at all those.

"Okay," Aly said, "I have our list. I think we should wait until we get home to give it to Mom, when she's more relaxed, you know?"

Brooke peeked out the door of the back room. There were tons of people in the salon. "I think so too," she said. "Come on. It looks like Carla and Joan could use our help."

Over the next two hours Aly cleaned up two broken bottles of nail polish (Green with Envy and Really Rosie), took out the trash three times (it was overflowing with the soft twisty paper that went between people's toes for pedicures), and went to the bank once to get one hundred dollars' worth of one-dollar bills so her mom could give people change.

In the meantime, Brooke ordered pizza for the

staff, fixed the nail polish display four times, and read *Big Dog, Little Dog* to Mrs. Fornari's two-year-old son. Three times in a row. Mrs. Fornari was a jewelry maker, and to thank Brooke, she gave her a box of extra beads and some leftover string that she had in her pocketbook.

"Aly!" Mom almost shouted when Aly came through the door with the money. "Thank goodness you're back! I need you to take over the phones."

Aly took her seat behind the desk and looked at the people still waiting. One was Jenica's friend Bethany, whom Aly recognized from school. Bethany walked over.

"Hello," Aly said, trying to be professional. "Do you want a magazine?"

"You're Aly, right?" Bethany said, ignoring the question.

Aly nodded. "Right."

"That's what I thought," Bethany said. "So instead of me waiting on this line, can you just give me a pedicure? At our game this morning Jenica said you're awesome at it, as long as your hair isn't in your eyes. And that you're really fast."

"I, um, I . . . ," Aly said, not really sure what to say. "You have to ask my mom?" is what she finally ended up with. It was kind of a babyish answer, but also a true one.

"Okay," Bethany said. "Which one's your mom?"

Whew. Bethany wasn't acting like Aly's answer was babyish.

"She's over there," Aly said, pointing. "The one with the same hair as me. In the blue shirt."

Bethany returned to the waiting area and spoke to a grown-up—probably her own mom. Then the woman went over to Aly's mom. And then Aly's mom got up from her station and walked over to Aly.

"Did you tell Bethany's mom to ask me if you could do her toes?" Mom asked. Aly could tell she wasn't happy.

"I didn't know what else to say," Aly answered, which was the total and complete truth. "She's a sixth grader," Aly added.

Aly's mom chewed on her lip for a moment, then sighed. "I know I keep breaking my own rules, but do you think you could give Bethany a pedicure? And Jenica's other friend should be here in fifteen minutes. Could you do her, too? Her name is Mia."

Aly couldn't believe it. She got to do two more pedicures and she hadn't gotten in trouble. Maybe it would be easier than she thought to convince Mom about the kid salon later.

Aly took Bethany to the back room, and Brooke followed with all the sparkle polishes.

"Thanks, Brooke," Aly said.

"Yeah, thanks," Bethany added.

Aly slipped a hair elastic off her wrist and pulled back the top half of her hair. She got down to cleaning and filing and polishing, and Brooke got down to chatting with Bethany. Aly was paying so much attention to Brooke's conversation about Sadie the dog and how famous she was that she almost spilled the bottle of Under Watermelon polish on Bethany's flip-flop. Luckily, she caught it just in time and Bethany didn't notice, and Aly quickly finished.

Brooke glanced into the main salon. "No free dryers," she reported. "But don't worry, I'll fan you."

She picked up two magazines and waved them back and forth over Bethany's toes.

"Thanks, you two," Bethany said. "Jenica was right—this was awesome."

Just then Mia appeared in the doorway.

"Hey," she said, cracking her gum. "Aly, right? Your mom said I should come back here."

"Mia!" Bethany squealed. "I didn't know you were coming too!"

Mia sat down next to Bethany. "Jenica's toes looked so cool. I think the whole soccer team should get them. Even though you can't see the sparkles with our socks and cleats on, we'll all know we have sparkle power underneath."

"Some other girls called today," Aly told them. "But we were booked."

"Overbooked is more like it," Mia said. "Did you see the crowd out there? I'm so glad I don't have to wait on that line."

Aly got to work while Mia and Bethany chatted. Brooke was still fanning, which made it hard for her to talk. Then Aly accidentally dipped the Orange You Pretty brush in the Strawberry Sunday bottle.

"Aly!" Brooke panted, her eyes huge. "Did you just . . ."

Aly blinked her eyes extremely hard, the Secret Sister Eye Message for *I know, but don't say it out loud!* Then she quickly wiped off the brush.

Brooke touched one of Bethany's toes carefully and pronounced her dry. Then she slid next to Aly. "Do you want me to open and close the polish bottles?" she whispered.

A polish assistant! Just what Aly needed. Sometimes having a sister really was the best thing in the world. Aly and Brooke worked together to finish the pedicure. Then both sisters took up fanning Mia's toes.

"We need some dryers back here," Brooke whispered. "My arms are getting tired."

Aly agreed. When Mia's nails were dry, both sixth graders stood up.

"Thanks so much," Bethany said as she was leaving.

"Yeah, thanks," Mia echoed. "This was a totally awesome pedicure. I'm going to tell the rest of the team that they *have* to come get some sparkle power."

"You're welcome," Aly and Brooke said together.

"And that would be great!" Brooke added.

Once they were alone, the sisters fell onto the small couch, exhausted but happy. "That was so much fun," Brooke said. "Even if my arms feel like noodles from all that fanning."

"You were right before," Aly said. "If Mom lets us have our own salon back here, we're going to need dryers—for fingers and for toes."

All of a sudden, Aly was extra worried about their salon. If Mom had to spend a lot of money to make it work, there was a big chance she'd turn them down.

That's why, a few hours later, after they'd closed

up the salon and were having dinner at Trattoria Spaghetto, Aly found herself unable to swallow her mouthful of meatball.

It didn't matter if Aly was able to talk or not, though. As usual, Brooke's mouth didn't stop going. While she was sucking down spaghetti, Brooke blurted out, "Mom, Aly and I have something important to ask you."

Aly managed to choke down her food. She pulled the list she and Brooke had made earlier out of the back pocket of her jean shorts.

"We, um," Aly said, unfolding the paper. "We, um, think that we could really help out at the salon if we, um . . ."

"We want to open our own kid salon!" Brooke said, bouncing up and down in her seat. "In the back room! And we'd do kids' nails and have parties and it would be good for True Colors because, because . . ."

Aly handed the paper to her mom. "It would be good because we could handle all the kids so you could polish even more grown-ups."

Mom looked at the girls' proposal. She read it over once. Then twice. Maybe even three times.

Brooke grabbed Aly's hand under the table. Aly's legs were jiggling hard. She couldn't stop them. *Say yes, say yes,* she thought.

But Mom sighed.

"This is a terrific idea, girls," she said. "It would be a big help to me and to the salon. I know I've asked Aly to give a few pedicures these last two days, but I can't agree to this."

"Why not?" Brooke asked, tears already filling her eyes. Aly felt like she wanted to cry too.

"Because your father and I have spoken about this before. We both agreed that schoolwork and being a kid should always come first for you two. That's why we both work so hard, why he travels all the time—so you two can focus on being children."

"But we don't want to be children," Brooke cried. "We want a salon."

Aly bit her lip. "What if we could do both?" she asked. "What if we could be children *and* run a salon?"

"I don't think so," Mom said, finishing the last of her chicken parmesan.

Aly and Brooke looked at each other. They couldn't eat another bite.

"Okay, kids," Mom said, leaving some money on the table. "It's been a long day. Let's go home."

On the way home, though, Aly had another idea—one she wouldn't tell Brooke, in case her sister opened her mouth again. She wasn't about to give up on the salon just yet. But she would have to wait until tomorrow to put her plan into action.

five

So Berry Blue

Beep, beep, beep.

Aly opened her eyes to the sound of the alarm on her purple polka-dot watch. It beeped softly from its spot underneath her pillow. She pulled it out and clicked it off: 6:45 a.m., just like she'd planned.

Super quietly, Aly slid out of her bed. She turned the doorknob really slowly so it wouldn't make its normal loud click and tiptoed down the hallway to the kitchen. She wished her parents would let her have a cell phone so she could make calls whenever and wherever she wanted, but that was another Tanner rule: No cell until middle school.

Right next to the toaster oven was the phone. Aly picked up it up and walked over to the back door—as far away from Mom's bedroom as possible. She dialed.

Ring, ring, ring.

Answer already, Aly thought anxiously.

"Hello?" a deep voice answered. "Honey? Is everything okay?"

"It's me, Dad," Aly whispered. "Not Mom. And everything's okay. Except for not exactly everything."

Aly leaned against the door, resting her head against the pale gray window shade.

"What do you mean?" Dad said, sounding worried.

"I mean—" Aly took a deep breath, and when she let it out, all the words came with it. "I mean that when you get home, you have to talk to Mom because Brooke and I don't care about our childhoods, and the thing we want to do most is polish other kids' nails at True Colors in the back room, and even if you and Mom don't want us to work, we want to, and also it'll teach us a lot of responsibility for when we're older, plus it'll help Mom out a lot at the salon because it's mega-busy and it's making her tired and also it'll be fun."

There was a pause on the other end of the phone. "So, you girls asked Mom, and she said no?"

Now there was a pause on Aly's end. "Yes," she said, in her smallest voice.

Dad sighed. "Let's talk about this when I'm home tonight," he said. "Okay?"

All of a sudden, Aly got a little excited inside. "You mean there's still hope?"

"There's always hope, Alligator, but I've got a plane to catch. We'll all talk later."

Her father said, "I love you." Aly did the same and beeped off. Then she crept back to her room, got into her bed, and closed her eyes. But she was much too excited to sleep. So she got her favorite purple pen and a piece of frog-shaped paper and started a new list, writing down all the things that she and Brooke would learn from running a salon, like how to be responsible and organized and patient. When Aly heard Mom turning the doorknob, she stuffed the list underneath her pillow and pretended to snore.

"Move George over, Brookie," Mom said after she'd opened the blinds to let the sun in. Brooke put her stuffed monkey on the night table, and Mom lay down next to her.

"Uh-oh," Aly said. "What's the matter? Is Dad okay?" She started to worry, even though he had sounded fine when she'd spoken to him earlier.

"Everything is fine, girls," Mom said. "But how about you don't come with me to the salon today? Aly, why don't you go swimming at the Y with Lily? And,

Brooke, there's an art class there at the same time."

Aly felt like someone had punched her in the stomach. No salon? But that was her favorite place in the world. It was where she belonged. Plus, she *hated* swim class. Mean Suzy Davis was there.

Before Aly could say anything, Brooke took matters into her own hands: She started crying. Wailing, really.

Mom tried to put her arms around Brooke, but Brooke turned to face the wall.

"Why are you being so *me-ean*?" Brooke hiccuped, still not looking at Mom. "First no k-kid salon, a-and now no Tr-rue Colors?"

"Brooke," Mom said. "Enough."

"It's *n-not* enough," Brooke sobbed.

"Really, Mom," Aly said. "We don't want go to the Y today. Especially not to go swimming. Please let us come. *Please?*"

Mom looked at her watch. Then she looked at Aly

and Brooke. Finally, she shook her head. "Fine," she said. "But now we're running late. Let's get a move on."

It took only three seconds for Brooke to stop crying. Aly was impressed—she could never stop crying that quickly. Once she got started, tears kept coming.

Three green lights and two stop signs later, the Tanners pulled up in front of True Colors.

Aly and Brooke ran to the front door, but Mom got out of the car and stopped. In the middle of the sidewalk. Staring at a glittery banner on the empty store across the street—the one that used to be a candy shop: COMING SOON! PRINCESS POLISH! A NAIL SALON FOR THE WHOLE FAMILY! When did that sign show up? It wasn't there yesterday!

Mom stared at it for three minutes, according to Aly's watch. Then her mouth made a really straight line, and she marched into True Colors without looking at the girls. Clearly, Mom was not having a very good morning.

"Why is another salon coming across the street?" Brooke asked Aly.

Aly shrugged. "I don't know. I guess they want to polish people's nails too."

"But," Brooke said, her lower lip wobbling, "but what if people like that salon better than ours? What if Mrs. Franklin stops coming? And Miss Lulu? And all the other regulars?"

Aly figured that's just what Mom was worried about—why she had stood so long on the sidewalk.

"I think we just have to make sure they don't," Aly said. "Here's the plan. We're going to do our jobs today the very best we can. If something might possibly go wrong, we're going to stop it before it does. We've got to make sure everyone knows True Colors is the best salon ever."

Six
Orange You Pretty

Later that afternoon, when the salon rush had slowed down a bit, Brooke, Aly, and Joan were having their traditional Sunday Pizza Picnic in the back room. The door to the main salon was open, and it was finally quiet enough to hear the background music over the hum of nail dryers and conversation. Aly couldn't help bopping her head a little while she chewed. When it was quiet like this, True Colors really felt like home.

"Want to trade your pepperoni for my mushrooms?" Brooke asked Joan.

"Sure thing," Joan answered, peeling three pieces of pepperoni off her pizza slice and handing them over.

Brooke popped them in her mouth and started laughing.

"What's so funny?" Joan asked. She looked over at Aly, but Aly shrugged. She had no idea why her nutball sister was having a fit about pepperoni.

"No pepperoni for Joanie!" Brooke laughed. "It rhymes!"

Joan smiled. "You mean like . . . no cookie for Brookie?"

Brooke stopped laughing immediately. "But . . . I get a cookie, right?"

Joan finished swallowing Brooke's mushrooms. "Of course you get a cookie. I'm testing out a new recipe. The rest of the manicurists are waiting for your verdict before they give it a go."

Aly loved Sunday Pizza Picnics. She loved that Joan brought them cookies to try. She even loved the way everyone else in the salon waited until Aly and Brooke gave a cookie two thumbs up before they ate it. Basically, Aly loved everything about True Colors.

"This is the best place in the world, isn't it?" Aly asked as Joan handed her a raspberry–peanut butter macaron.

"Absolutely!" Brooke said, snuggling next to Joan and taking a cookie from the tin.

Aly let her head rest against Joan's other shoulder.

"So what do you think?" Joan asked as the girls bit into the cookies.

"It tastes like you turned a peanut butter and jelly sandwich into a cookie." Brooke said, looking up at Joan. "How did you do that?"

"A baker never tells her secrets." Joan winked. "What do you think, Aly?"

Aly let the taste of the cookie settle on her tongue. "This is what I like about it," she said. "One, it's salty and sweet at the same time. Two, the peanut butter part is really creamy. Three, there's a little bit of crunch to the outside of the cookie. And four, it's big enough that you need four bites to finish it."

"Thank you for that wonderful list," Joan said. "I'll tell the rest of the ladies that these cookies have the Aly-and-Brooke Seal of Approval."

"Hey, Aly?" someone said from the doorway.

Aly looked up. It was Jenica! And Bethany and Mia. There were three more girls from the soccer team behind them.

"Any chance you can polish some more toes when you're done eating?" Jenica asked.

Aly stood up and swallowed her last bite of cookie. "We're all booked today," she said. She really wasn't sure if they were totally booked, but she didn't want to have to ask Mom to break her rules again . . . not yet, anyway.

Jenica put her hands on her hips. "You know, you and your mom always say that, but then you take people in here and give them pedicures. Can we just skip to that part?"

"Um . . ." Aly didn't have a choice—she looked into the main salon for her mom.

"How about if I go see if Karen is back?" Joan said, squeezing Aly's shoulder. "And if not, I'll come back here and we'll figure this out." Aly nodded, grateful, as always, for Joan.

"Mia and Bethany and I played awesome yesterday after you gave us the sparkle pedicures," Jenica said. "We have another game after school tomorrow. And we really need to win. So our starting forwards need pedicures too."

Jenica introduced the girls who had followed her

in: Giovanna, Maxie, and Joelle. They looked a little familiar to Aly from school, but she'd never spoken to any of them before.

Aly found it kind of amazing that the girls thought her sparkle pedicure made them play soccer better. She wondered if she'd be a soccer star if she painted her own toenails.

"Aly's not allowed to," Brooke said as she cleaned up the Pizza Picnic. "Really. Unless our mom says it's okay, and she's not here right now."

"There she is!" Mia said from behind Jenica.

Mom came walking toward the back room, carrying a bag from the grocery store. "Can I help you girls?" she asked as she slid the bag into the mini-fridge.

"Our friends need three rainbow sparkle pedicures," Jenica said. "Otherwise, we won't win our soccer game. But Aly said you're booked. Like she always does."

Bethany leaned in and whispered to Mia, "Maybe we should just go to another salon today." Even though she whispered, Aly could tell that Mom heard; her eyes darted toward the front window and the COMING SOON! PRINCESS POLISH! sign across the street.

"Aly," Mom said, "can I talk to you, please?"

Aly followed her mother into the corner near the two spare manicure stations stored in the back room.

"I'm *not* agreeing to your salon," Mom said. "But would you do three more pedicures? Or see if Brooke can do one? I want to make sure everyone is happy with our salon today."

Aly grinned. It wasn't a guarantee, but it seemed like the first step in making their own kid salon a reality. "Okay, Mom," she said.

After leading Maxie and Joelle to the pedicure chairs and turning on the water, Aly pulled Brooke over near the mini-fridge for a chat.

"I've never done a real customer before," Brooke said, tugging on her braid. "I don't even do both of your hands! Just one! Are you sure I'm ready for this?"

Lisa, another manicurist, walked into the back room to grab a bottle of water and heard the girls' conversation.

"You're going to be great," Lisa said. "Just take your time and go slow. Aly can do two of the girls. You only have to do one."

Brooke nodded, but she didn't seem convinced.

"Okay," Aly said, walking back to the pedicure chairs, "so, um, after you're done splashing, I'm going to do Maxie's toes, and Brooke will do Joelle's. Then I'll do Giovanna's. Sound good?"

Brooke smiled, but she wrapped her hand around the bottom of her braid so she could tug it if she had to.

"You're sure your sister can do it?" Jenica asked,

folding her arms across her chest. "She's just a little kid."

"We're all kids," Brooke told Jenica. "And I bet I can polish a million times better than you."

Aly swallowed hard. She couldn't believe Brooke. One of the main rules in a salon is never to be mean to the customers! Brooke was going to ruin this!

But instead of getting mad, Jenica laughed. So did Joelle. "I like her," she said.

"Why, thank you," Brooke answered, and even curtsied. Then she ducked outside to get the sparkle polishes. Jenica, Bethany, and Mia followed her out the door.

All three pedicures proceeded pretty much problem-free. Brooke was concentrating so hard on her work that she didn't say a word, but she still had to redo the Orange You Pretty on Joelle's pointer toe twice because it kept dripping. Once all the girls' toes were dry, though, they left with huge smiles on their faces.

Right before they walked out the door, Giovanna said, "If we win tomorrow, we're coming back every week. And we're bringing the rest of the team too."

"Sounds good," Aly said, smiling her biggest smile. But a list of worries started in her brain: How would True Colors handle the whole sixth-grade soccer team every week for pedicures? Would there be enough open spots? Maybe customers would actually want to go to Princess Polish across the street. Aly and Brooke couldn't let that happen.

Aly reached into her back pocket and pulled out the list she'd made on the frog paper that morning. She folded it in half and wrote *For Mom and Dad* on the front. Then she opened the closet in the back room where Mom kept her purse and taped the note to Mom's house key. That way, she wouldn't miss it.

Later that night Aly and Brooke were sitting on the floor of their bedroom in their pj's, rubbing cotton balls dipped in polish remover across their Go for the Gold nails.

"It's a shame we have to take it off," Aly said. "Mine's barely chipped."

"I know," Brooke said, fluttering her fingers. "Look how it sparkles. I think our family has too many rules. Other kids are allowed to wear nail polish to school. And our mom has a nail salon! I mean, if *anyone* should get to wear polish, it's us, right?"

"Right." Aly was listening to Brooke, but she was also thinking about rules. And the piece of paper taped to Mom's key chain. Dad was due home any minute from the airport and Aly was hoping he and Mom would read the list together.

"Let's pretend . . . ," Brooke said, dipping her cotton ball in more polish remover. "Let's pretend that we have our own salon. What would we name it?"

There was a knock on their bedroom door, and both girls looked up.

"Daddy!" Brooke was on her feet and racing toward Dad's legs.

Aly stood up too, waiting her turn for a hug. But before she could even get her chance with Dad, Mom walked in behind him and started talking.

"So we've made a decision, girls," she said, slipping her arm around Dad's waist.

Aly's stomach did a cartwheel.

"We know how much it means to you two, and we know how responsible and helpful you both have been at True Colors, so, after a long, long talk, we've decided . . . that you can have your own salon!"

Brooke started screeching and jumping around the room. "We can do it! We can do it!" she yelled.

Aly was stunned. She just stood there, smiling.

Everything she'd been wishing for was going to come true! Mom and Dad had said yes!

Brooke jumped over and threw her arms around her sister. Finally, Aly jumped with her. "We can do it!" Aly whispered. "I can't believe we can do it!"

"Don't get too excited yet," Mom said. "There are lots of rules."

But Aly didn't care if there were a thousand million rules. She and Brooke were going to get their own salon!

seven
Red-Hot Pepper

Monday mornings were always a mad rush in the Tanner house—Dad usually had to leave on a new trip, the girls had school, Mom had the salon, and they all had to be out of the house much earlier than they would have liked. Plus, they couldn't forget backpacks or school lunches or briefcases or pocketbooks.

This Monday was no exception. Usually, Dad drove the girls to school on Mondays himself, but today Mom hopped into the car too. Once they pulled out of the driveway, Mom turned around and handed Aly and Brooke each an envelope. "These are the rules I was talking about," she said. "And there are a lot of them."

Aly looked at the list.

Rules for Aly and Brooke's Salon

- Aly and Brooke may polish only kids' nails.
- Aly and Brooke may polish nails only three days a week: two school days and one weekend day.
- All homework must be done before their salon can open for business.
- Aly and Brooke may not charge clients. Instead, there will be a donation jar. After the cost of supplies is covered, the rest of the money will be donated to any charity of Aly and Brooke's choice.
- Aly and Brooke will be on probation for one week before the salon becomes official.

Probation? That was one of Aly's spelling bee words. But she couldn't remember the definition.

"What's that word?" Brooke whispered.

Aly shook her head. "Mom," she asked, "what do you mean by 'probation,' and why do we have to be on it?"

Mom twisted around to face the girls. "It means we're going to use this week as a test run."

Aly took a deep breath. A test! This would be hard. But they had to try it.

"Okay," Aly said. "We're okay with your list."

Brooke nodded her agreement.

"Then look at the bottom of the papers," Mom said.

Aly saw a blank line with *Alyssa Tanner* printed beneath it. Brooke's paper had the same line, but with *Brooke Tanner* underneath.

"Here's a pen. I need you to sign these papers, to prove that you understand the rules."

Aly had never signed anything official other than the electronic package machine for Arnold. She took a pen and signed her name in her neatest handwriting. Then she handed the pen to Brooke, who did the same, drawing a flower next to it.

"Okay, done," Brooke said. "We're signed. What do we do now?"

"Congratulations, girls," Dad said, glancing at them in the rearview mirror. "You are now salon operators! But first you have school. Time to go."

Aly and Brooke got out of the car and ran in different directions toward their classes.

Aly couldn't believe it. Her biggest dream had just come true. Even with all the rules.

"Hey, Nail Polish Aly!" someone called from the other side of the hallway.

Aly looked up. It was Jenica, with a group of soccer girls. Jenica had never spoken to Aly at school before. Was she really talking to her now?

"Me?" Aly asked, immediately feeling silly for saying it. Of course Jenica meant her. What other Alys were there in school who polished nails?

"We had a scrimmage yesterday after the forwards got their pedicures," Jenica said, "just to see if the sparkle pedicure really worked. And every single person who had your rainbow polish either scored a goal or blocked a goal. We think we need you and your sister to do the rest of the team before our game next weekend."

Aly could barely answer, she was so excited. Today, she and Brooke wouldn't be at True Colors, so she told Jenica to call the salon tomorrow afternoon and she would make the team appointments. Maybe the soccer team would be the first real customers for the kid salon!

The bell rang, and Aly headed into her classroom. The morning was pretty regular: Aly sat between

Garrett and Cameron, who were pretty cool for boys. And during art class she got to work on a scratchboard art project with her best school friend, Lily. Her other best school friend, Charlotte, and Charlotte's twin brother, Caleb, were doing their own scratchboard project at the other end of the table.

Everything was going smoothly . . . until lunch.

Aly was sitting between Lily and Charlotte, about to take a bite of her peanut butter sandwich when Brooke came running over. Third-grade recess was just ending, so Brooke had only a few minutes to talk.

"Guess what! Guess what!" she said, her braid flying behind her.

"Are you okay?" Aly asked automatically.

"*More* than okay!" Brooke said. "I booked us a ton of appointments and also a birthday party!"

"You booked us a *what*?" Aly choked out.

"It's for this first grader, Heather, who I sometimes

jump rope with. Her birthday's tomorrow, and she wasn't going to have a party on the actual day. Her parents are doing one for her over the weekend, but her babysitter told her yesterday that she could have an actual day party too! She didn't know what kind of party to have, so I told her about our salon, and she's going to have her party there. Tomorrow!"

Aly was speechless for a second. Then she said, "We have to check with Mom. We're on probation, remember? What if Mom doesn't want us to do a party yet? We didn't even decide if we were working tomorrow!"

"Well, she'll have to say yes. I already booked it," Brooke answered, like it wasn't a big deal.

Aly closed her eyes to focus her thoughts. "*Whose* party did you say we were doing?"

"Heather," Brooke said. "Heather Davis. I think her sister's in your grade."

All of a sudden, Aly felt kind of pukey. "You agreed to do Suzy Davis's sister's party?"

Maybe she said it a little louder than she meant to, because Brooke's eyes started filling up with tears. "I thought it was a good thing to book a birthday party! It's only a few girls. Why are you getting so upset?"

"No, it's fine, it's fine," Aly said, giving her sister a hug. "I just . . . um . . . I'm not really friends with Suzy. Not that it matters. But it's fine. We'll give Heather a great birthday party."

Aly gave Brooke another hug, and then Brooke ran off toward the third-grade hallway. Once she was gone, Aly laid her head down on the lunch table.

Lily moved her chair closer to Aly's. "Did I hear that right? Are you going to be polishing Heather Davis's nails for her birthday?"

"Yes," Aly said into the table.

"You don't think Suzy will be there, do you?" Lily asked. "And will want her nails polished too?"

"Yes and yes," Aly said, still muttering into her lunch. "I can't believe Brooke did this."

"It sounds like she was just trying to help," Charlotte said.

"I know." Aly finally lifted her head. "But this is the worst kind of helping possible. And I have a feeling my mom's going to be mad. *Really* mad. And we don't even have a real salon set up yet. It's just a back room, with a refrigerator and lots of boxes in it. What kind of party will that be?"

Lily offered Aly a chocolate chip cookie. Aly took it and crammed the whole thing into her mouth at once. But it would take more than a chocolate chip cookie to make this day better. And tomorrow? "I think I need another cookie, Lily," Aly said. "Or six."

eight
Silver Celebration

On Tuesday afternoon at four o'clock, Heather Davis and her partyers appeared.

Heather's babysitter sat down for her manicure with Lisa, and the three party girls started dancing around the salon, talking and laughing and coming dangerously close to knocking things over. As Aly had suspected, her mom was already not very happy that they'd agreed to host a birthday party without talking to her first.

"You have to keep them under control," Mom said

quietly to Aly. "I said you could have your own salon, but you have to remember that this is a business. My business. And your salon can't cause problems for my customers."

Aly gulped. "I promise, Mom. Brooke and I can handle it." Really, they had no other choice. Otherwise, their salon was doomed.

"Okay, birthday-party people," Aly said. "If you want your nails polished, follow Brooke through that door!"

The three girls started marching behind Brooke. After grabbing a handful of nail polish colors, Aly joined them in the back room. Brooke was in front of the pedicure basins, turning on the water.

"Who wants to choose a polish color?" Aly asked.

The girls came running.

Aly held out the colors she'd grabbed: Red-Hot

Pepper, Silver Celebration, Orange You Pretty, and Pinkie Swear.

"I want the red!" the girl with the headband said.

"No, *I* want red!" the other girl said.

"You can both have the same color," Aly told them.

"But *I* want red! Just me," Heather said, her voice starting to wobble. "And I'm the birthday girl."

Brooke walked over to Heather's two guests. "You know what I think would be perfect on you guys?" She picked up the sparkly silver bottle. "Silver Celebration. Look how glittery it is! And today's Heather's birthday celebration, so even the name is perfect. What do you think, Tali?" she asked the girl with the headband.

Tali examined it. "I like sparkles," she said.

"Jayden?" Brooke asked the other girl.

"I like sparkles too," Jayden said.

"Great!" Brooke said. "And, Heather, you can have Red-Hot Pepper."

Heather smiled. It was the kind of smile that changed her whole face. "Me first."

Aly let out a breath she didn't know she'd been holding. Maybe they could do this after all. "Actually, I think we can do all three of you together. Tali and Jayden will just have to share a chair."

Aly led the three girls to the chairs and told them to climb on. But she forgot to tell them to take off their shoes first, and Heather's flip-flop fell right into the water.

"Oh no!" Heather said, and promptly jumped off the chair *into* the water to get it. Now both of her flip-flops were wet! It was a good thing she was wearing shorts or her pants would've gotten soaked.

Aly helped Heather back into the chair and wrapped her flip-flops in towels so they'd dry faster.

If she and Brooke had their own toe dryers back here, she would've stuck them in there. But for now, towels were the best she could manage.

"So I'll do you," Aly told Heather, "and Brooke will do Tali."

"Who's going to do me?" Jayden asked.

"Both of us," Brooke told her.

Jayden seemed intrigued by that.

Aly kneeled down next to the pedicure basin to get to work, but it turned out that first graders are much squirmier than sixth graders.

"That tickles!" Heather squealed when Aly rubbed soap on her feet. But she didn't just say it, she also kicked water on Aly's shirt.

Brooke took a break from working on Tali to explain the bite-your-tongue-so-you-won't-feel-the-tickle trick, which made things a little better, but Heather was still pretty wiggly. Aly had to hold on to her feet super tightly to keep the polish in the right place.

"Hey, you got it on my skin!" Aly heard Tali say to Brooke as she wiggled in the chair.

Brooke cleaned off the polish and told her, "You've got to try to stay still, or that's going to keep happening."

"I can't help it!" Tali said. "It's hard to sit still."

"Is it my turn yet?" Jayden asked.

Aly looked around to find something for Jayden to do. Her eyes fell on the box of beads and the string that Mrs. Fornari had given Brooke.

She quickly opened the box of beads and handed it to Jayden. "While you're waiting to get your nails done, you get to make a bracelet. You can use any color beads you want," she said.

"Wait!" said Brooke. "I just had a better idea. *Everyone* can make bracelets. Ankle bracelets, actually, since they're bigger. That way, you'll have something to do in the chair to help you stop jiggling."

Brooke quickly cut three lengths of string and gave one to each girl, telling them to knot one end so the beads wouldn't slip off. The girls all starting beading. And they finally sat still! And Heather bit her tongue so she wasn't ticklish. This party was turning out okay after all.

Aly finished up Heather's Red-Hot Pepper toes just as Brooke finished up Tali's Silver Celebration pedi. "One foot each?" Brooke said, handing a second bottle of Silver Celebration to Aly.

"Great idea." Aly smiled.

Working as a team, the sisters finished Jayden's toes in no time. All three girls worked on their bracelets as their nails dried.

"So," Aly asked, "how do you like your toes?"

"Mine are beautiful," Jayden said, wiggling them and watching them sparkle.

"Mine too," Tali agreed, glancing down at her feet.

"I"—Heather sniffled—"I hate mine! Red-Hot Pepper is the worst color ever!" And she burst into tears.

Aly looked at Brooke in a panic. Brooke was looking panicked too.

"Um," Aly said. "Wait—we can redo it. Do you want Silver Celebration like your friends?"

Heather shook her head. "I want a sp-special birthday c-color."

"How about . . . Under Watermelon? Or Strawberry Sunday? Those are both really sparkly," Brooke said.

"Not red or pink," Heather said, wiping her eyes. "Something even more special."

"My favorite's Purple People Eater," Aly offered. "How about that one?"

"That's a scary name," Heather said. "I don't want one with a scary name."

Brooke's favorite was Pinkie Swear, which didn't

have a scary name but wouldn't work anyway, because Heather didn't want pink.

Brooke's eyes opened wide. "Hold on," she said.

She ran out into the main salon and came back with two bottles of Lemon Aid, bright yellow *and* super sparkly.

Heather stopped crying.

Since teamwork had worked so well with Jayden, Aly and Brooke did it again.

"What do you think *now*?" Brooke asked when they'd finished.

"I think they're beautiful!" Heather couldn't stop staring at her feet. "They're the brightest, sparkliest toes I've ever seen."

Brooke gathered up the cotton balls and nail polish bottles. "We did it," she whispered to Aly.

Aly opened the pedicure basin drains. "Nice job," she whispered back.

Then there was a knock at the door. "Okay, girls, party's over," Aly said, heading over to let in Heather's babysitter.

But when she opened the door, it was Suzy Davis.

"You have a silver splotch on your leg," Suzy said.

Aly looked down. Sure enough, there was silver nail polish there, in the shape of a very small banana.

"Oh," she said. "Thanks."

"I came to get my sister and her friends," Suzy said. "But before we go, I want a pedicure too."

Was Aly really going to have to polish Suzy's toes? Heather's birthday party had been hard enough. And now this?

"I'd like a rainbow," Suzy said. "With . . . with hearts painted on each toe. In opposite colors."

Opposite colors? What did that even mean?

"It's the first day of our salon," Brooke said from behind Aly. "We're closed now. This was just a test run. Our grand opening is set for another day. You can come back then."

Sometimes Aly had no idea where Brooke came up with this stuff.

"Who are you?" Suzy said.

"Aly's sister Brooke," Brooke answered. "Who are you?"

Aly looked over at Heather and her friends. They were still admiring their feet.

"I'm Heather's sister, and I want a rainbow pedicure. Aly's going to give me one."

"No," said Brooke, "she isn't. If you want a rainbow pedicure, please make an appointment in the main salon with one of those manicurists. I said we're closed." Her hands were on her hips now.

Brooke looked at Aly and gave her a Secret Sister Eye Message. Aly gave her one back: *Thank you, thank you, thank you.*

"What if I tell your mom that you won't give me a pedicure?" Suzy's hands were on her hips now too.

"This is our salon," Aly said, finally finding her voice and stepping forward. "You can try telling our mom that, but it won't make a difference. We have our own rules here."

Suzy looked hard at Aly. She looked at Brooke. And back at Aly.

Then she looked around the back room. "Everyone at school was saying how great this place is. But it's kind of gross. I'm going to tell everyone it's a dump. And that they should go to the place across the street when it opens. This place is fine for first graders, but no one else would ever step foot in here." Suzy walked over to her sister and her sister's two friends. "Come on, let's go," she said.

Next thing Aly knew, Suzy, Heather, and the

rest of the girls were leaving the back room. As they walked out, Aly heard them talking.

"This was the coolest birthday party ever!" Tali said to Jayden. "I want it for my birthday. It's February first. Can you come?"

Aly smiled. Well, at least Tali had had a good time.

And then she heard Suzy say to Heather. "Hey, your toes look pretty. Nice color."

Well, that was interesting. Aly hadn't expected Suzy to say anything nice about the salon.

But then Aly remembered the other things Suzy had said. And as she looked around the back room, Aly realized Suzy was right. It *was* a bit of a dump, filled with boxes and water bottles and mismatched everything. If this place was going to be a hit, they'd need to do some redecorating. Otherwise, like Suzy said, their only customers would be first graders.

nine

Teal Me the Truth

Since Dad was back on the road, dinner was going to be just the girls. But Aly wasn't interested in food at all.

Besides worrying about how Mom was going to react to the unofficial first day of the salon before the grand opening, Aly also couldn't stop thinking about what Suzy had said. The back room really did look more like a huge storage closet than someplace special.

If they couldn't make it look really cool and

inviting, they wouldn't get any customers—well, except for maybe the sixth-grade soccer team. But they'd need more clients than that to make the salon real.

By the time they'd gotten home from True Colors, it was later than usual for a school night. So Mom made "breakfast for dinner." It was super fast to make—eggs, toast, tiny sausages, and sliced-up orange smiles. Aly and Brooke sat down at their usual spots at the kitchen table, next to each other. Aly pressed her left leg against Brooke's right one. For courage.

"Okay, girls," Mom said when she sat down.

Aly braced herself for trouble. Instead, Mom gave them a few more rules that were actually helpful: All appointments made at school had to be written down and then run by Mom before they were confirmed. No more parties until they got the salon up and running smoothly. And they couldn't forget about the charity donations. (Heather and her friends had not donated. But that might have been because Aly and Brooke had forgotten to ask them to donate.)

With their stomachs full of breakfast for dinner, Brooke and Aly went up to their room.

"Okay, so what can we do to make our salon look better?" Brooke asked. "I don't want our grand opening to wind up as our grand closing."

Other than the two teal pedicure chairs and the two blue manicure stations, everything in the back room was pretty much the same shade of Chocolate Brownies, which, even though it had a tasty-sounding name, was the girls' least favorite polish color ever.

"Let me get some paper," Aly said. "I think we're going to need a list."

The girls brainstormed:

- Curtains
- Paintings/pictures for the walls
- Cushions for the manicure and pedicure chairs
- Rugs
- Special floor pillows for when people make bracelets in the drying area
- A beautiful, fancy donation jar
- Signs that tell people about the donations
- A shelf to display nail polishes
- A sign for the door

Brooke looked at the list. "We're missing one thing," she said. "A name! Our salon needs a name!"

Brooke was right.

"Any ideas?" Aly asked.

Brooke shrugged. "Maybe . . . Twinkle Toes?"

Aly made a face. "We do manicures, too."

Brooke tucked one braid behind her ear. "I'll keep thinking."

The girls went downstairs to show Mom the list. She agreed to everything except the curtains and the rugs. And she offered to let the girls go on a treasure hunt in the attic for cushions and pillows and shelves.

Aly and Brooke hadn't been in the attic for ages. All they remembered was that it was kind of dark. And that whenever Mom or Dad wanted to store something there, they would usually just pull down the ladder and throw stuff up on the landing.

Aly grabbed Brooke's hand as Mom pulled the creaky ladder down from the ceiling. A duffel bag came tumbling out and landed on Mom's head.

Mom dropped it on the floor next to her. "Take that as a warning," she said. "It's going to be pretty messy."

Mom climbed up slowly until her head disappeared

from view. "Can one of you girls flick on the light?"

Brooke was right next to the light switch and turned it on. The attic looked like it was glowing.

"Come on up, girls!" Mom shouted down.

With the hand that wasn't holding Brooke's, Aly grabbed the railing tightly. The ladder creaked with each step.

Aly imagined finding mountains of colorful pillows and cushions and shiny new shelves. It was okay if the attic was a mess as long as it was filled with treasures.

But when she got to the top of the ladder, Aly was shocked. There wasn't anything new and shiny about the attic. Just dust and piles of junk all over the place.

From right behind her, Brooke whispered, "We'll never find anything cool up here."

But then Mom laughed. "Look at this!" she said. She had lifted a dusty flowered bedsheet off a table and picked up an old cookie jar shaped like a strawberry.

"That's perfect for the donation jar," Brooke said, getting excited.

"Where did you even get that, Mom?" Aly asked, taking a few steps closer to the craziest-looking cookie jar she'd ever seen. The strawberry was enormous enough for the giant in "Jack and the Beanstalk," and it was painted a sparkly teal.

Mom flipped the jar over. "See these initials?" she said, showing the girls the *KB* at the bottom of the jar. "They're mine. Karen Benson. I made it in art school. I remember this color—it was called Teal Me the Truth. I used it because I loved the name so much."

"*You* went to art school?" Brooke said. Her eyes were huge. "How come you never told us?"

Mom's cheeks turned pink. She hugged the sparkly

strawberry to her stomach. "I never finished."

She never finished? Aly couldn't believe it. Her mom *always* finished what she started. It made Aly think something bad had happened back then. "Why not?" she asked softly.

"There wasn't enough money. I needed to get a job and couldn't concentrate on my classes after that. So I left."

Wow. That was too bad. And sad. And maybe it was part of the reason why Mom was so serious about the girls paying attention to school and not working when they were kids.

"*I* want to go to art school," Brooke said. "And make strawberries like this."

"Maybe you can," Mom said, putting the cookie jar down in a safe corner of the attic. "But that's a long way away. Let's keep hunting. What else do you girls need?"

"Floor pillows," Aly said, remembering the list in her head. "And cushions. Oh, and paintings for the walls, too." As they started looking around some more, Aly realized that the attic wasn't as much of a mess as it first appeared. She got into the treasure-hunting spirit with Brooke, peeking underneath sheets and inside boxes.

After about twenty minutes, Aly, Brooke, and Mom had found four striped floor pillows, one set of shelves, two polka-dot seat cushions, and four paintings Mom had made in art school—two of the sun, one of the moon, and one of a rainbow.

"Mom, these are beautiful," Aly said. "Can we hang them in our salon?"

"They're one hundred percent perfect, Mom! Please?" Brooke pleaded.

Mom nodded. "Of course," she said, blushing. "I'm glad you like them."

"Maybe you should paint some more," Aly suggested. "It doesn't matter that you're not in art school."

Mom shrugged. "I don't know about that," she said. "I'm busy enough as it is."

Aly made a note in her brain that maybe she and Brooke should get Mom some paint and art canvases for her birthday.

As the Tanner women continued their hunt. Brooke kept coming up with salon names. Nonstop, as usual. Aly found some of Mom's old art supplies— some heavy sketch paper and pastels. They weren't in great shape anymore, but they'd do perfectly well for making signs.

"One more name," Brooke said. "How about the Glitter Girls' Salon?"

Even Mom wrinkled her nose at that one.

But everything else seemed like it was falling into

place. And Mom and the girls agreed that the grand opening would be this Saturday.

School moved slower than a baby snail on Wednesday, Thursday, and Friday. Even dodgeball, Aly's favorite gym game, seemed to take forever. And Brooke said that recess felt like it lasted a million hours.

But kids did keep coming up to Aly and Brooke, asking all about their salon and when it would be open for business.

Every afternoon for those three days, Brooke met Aly at 3:00 on the dot. They hurried over to True Colors, finished their homework, and then worked on the salon redecoration.

On Wednesday they hung Mom's four pictures on the walls—with some help from Joan and Carla. And they found ways to hide all the boxes of supplies as best they could, piled under tables and stacked in out-of-the-way corners of the room.

On Thursday they set up a drying area near the couch, with magazines stored in a crate they'd found and pillows and a table for a jewelry-making station. Then they created a polish display with the shelves from the attic.

On Friday they made a bunch of signs and taped them in all the right spots around them. Well, all the signs except for the one with the salon's name on it. They still hadn't settled on that. So while they worked, Brooke kept making suggestions, like Project Polish and Pretty Nails and Finger Fun. Also, Mermaid Manicures and Rainbow Polish and Tip-Top Nails. And Perfect Ten and Polish Palace and Happy Feet. Nothing seemed quite right, though.

As a finishing touch, they put the sparkly cookie jar on its own special table right next to the nail polish display. That way, no one would miss it.

"I can't believe how great this place looks," Brooke told Aly on Friday at closing time, as they stood in the doorframe admiring their work. "Now all we need to do is figure out a name!"

"And get some customers," Aly added.

And hope that know-it-all Suzy Davis wasn't right again.

ten

Power to the Sparkle

Should we put out all the colors for the rainbow pedicures?" Brooke asked. She was pulling on her braid so hard that Aly wondered how it wasn't hurting her.

"Sure," Aly said. "Let's put out two sets."

It was Saturday morning, the day of their grand opening. Aly was nervous too—she kept checking her polka-dot watch over and over. Jenica's entire soccer team was supposed to be coming in three minutes so they could all get rainbow pedicures before their afternoon game.

"Do you think the jewelry station looks okay?" Brooke asked. She'd spent the last fifteen minutes moving things around, changing the angle of the table and which pillow went where.

"I think it looks fine," Aly told her, checking her watch again. One minute. She went through the salon's preparation list in her head one last time. Everything was all set and ready to go. Well, except for the name. Brooke had been mad when Aly rejected Glimmering Good Salon and Magical Manicures earlier that morning, but Mom said that they shouldn't rush it, that the perfect name would come to them in time. Aly really hoped it would come soon.

She was looking at her watch when there was a knock on the door. Aly opened it. Nine girls stood in front of her, with Jenica at the front of the pack.

"Welcome," Aly tried to say, but it came out more like a swallow. She tried again. "Welcome to our salon." Then she stepped aside to let everyone walk in.

"Looks nice in here," Jenica said. "Much better than last time."

"Totally better," said Bethany.

Brooke still had her hand wrapped tightly around her hair, but she wasn't too nervous to talk. "This is the jewelry-making station," she said. "While you're waiting for your pedicure or for your polish to dry, you can make an ankle bracelet."

"We can't wear those," one of the girls said. "Because of our soccer socks. And shin guards."

"We can wear jewelry on our wrists, though," Jenica said, rolling her eyes. "We'll just make regular bracelets. It'll be great."

"That's right. You can make regular bracelets there too," Brooke said, smiling a tiny bit.

Aly took a deep breath. It was time to take charge. "Okay," she said, "let's get started."

Aly put the girls in groups of two, giving everyone instructions.

"Anjuli can go alone," Jenica said, pointing to a girl with a French braid longer than Brooke's. "She's our goalie, so she needs to get her fingernails painted too."

"In a rainbow?" Aly asked. It wasn't a problem—she'd be happy to paint Anjuli's fingers, she just needed to know the plan.

"I think maybe I want something different for my fingers," Anjuli said.

Brooke was standing in front of the polish display. "Why don't you come over here and pick your favorite color?" she said to Anjuli. "Aly and I can paint any color you want."

Anjuli walked over and started examining the display, but then she pointed to the strawberry donation jar.

"What's this?" she asked.

"That's our donation jar," Aly said. "Since no one has to pay in our salon, we're asking for donations instead. Whatever you decide to give, we'll donate to a charity once we have"—Aly did some fast thinking—"one hundred dollars. Every time we get to one hundred, we'll give it to a different charity."

"That's really cool," Bethany said.

The other girls nodded and unzipped their backpacks, looking for dollar bills and coins.

"Okay," Jenica said, "let's get going. We have a game to play this afternoon. We don't want to be here all day."

But even as she said it, she was smiling at Aly. Like she probably wouldn't mind if they were.

Jenica sat down on the couch and picked up a string and some beads. The other girls followed her to the waiting area, except for Maxie and Joelle, who were going first. The two forwards sat down in the pedicure chairs, and Aly and Brooke got started.

"Did you know Cute Lucas has a crush on Maria?" Joelle asked Maxie.

"No way!" Maxie answered. "Is he going to ask her to the Halloween dance?"

"Why do you call him Cute Lucas?" Brooke asked.

"Because Maxie thinks he's really handsome," Joelle answered.

"I do not!" Maxie said. "Okay, fine, I do. But you do, too!"

Maxie and Joelle started laughing. So did Aly and Brooke.

The first two pedicures went pretty smoothly, though there were a few times when Brooke needed to use the wooden stick with polish remover on it.

When Joelle and Maxie moved over to the drying area, Bethany and a girl whose name Aly didn't know took their places in the chairs.

"Hi, I'm Aly," Aly said while she was filling the basin with fresh water.

"I'm Valentina," the girl answered.

Valentina, it turned out, was ticklish and needed to hear about the tongue trick.

"You really want me to bite my tongue?" she asked.

"Not hard," Aly told her.

"It works!" Jenica piped in.

Valentina bit her tongue, and everything went well from there.

As the other girls got polished, Aly and Brooke listened to them chat about their strategy for the soccer game, their Halloween dance costumes, and which teachers gave the hardest sixth-grade math tests. The girls seemed really comfortable, and Aly and Brooke started feeling comfortable too, just like they did when they were hanging out in Mom's salon.

Brooke had just done the first coat of rainbow

polish on Giovanna and was getting ready for round two when Giovanna looked down at her. "I love how this looks," she said. "Maybe I'll keep coming even after soccer season."

Brooke looked up. "I didn't even know soccer girls liked sparkles until Jenica came to the salon."

"Just because we're good athletes doesn't mean we don't like sparkles," Giovanna said.

"Exactly," said Jenica.

"Definitely," said Mia, who was in Aly's chair now. "Girls can be smart, strong, *and* sparkly."

Aly liked that idea. Smart. And strong. And sparkly. She made a brain note to work on that.

After Giovanna and Mia were done, it was finally Anjuli's turn.

"I can do hands while you do feet," Brooke said to Aly.

"Fine," Aly said.

"Which color did you pick for your manicure?" Brooke asked Anjuli.

"Power to the Sparkle," she said, handing over a bottle.

"The multicolor glitter is really cool," Aly commented from where she was crouched, painting Anjuli's big toe.

"So," Anjuli said, "are you guys going to do this for us each week, for luck?"

Aly stopped polishing. "Well, as long as you guys want to keep coming, sure."

"As long as we keep winning, we keep coming!" Jenica said from the couch.

"Totally!" Bethany said.

"Power to the Sparkle!" Anjuli shouted.

"Power to the Sparkle!" Mia repeated.

Then they all started chanting, "Power to the Sparkle! Power to the Sparkle!"

Aly looked at Brooke and smiled. Brooke was grinning too. They didn't need any Secret Sister Eye Messages to know that their salon was off to a spectacular start.

That night the girls sat in their bedroom, counting the money from the donation jar.

"Seven dollars and thirty-one—no, thirty-two—cents," Aly announced.

After the soccer team had left, Lily and Charlotte showed up for manicures *and* pedicures, and then Brooke's friend Sophie and a few other third graders had come in for just pedicures. And then a couple of people who saw the sign in the True Colors window for the grand opening of a kids' salon.

"Do you think we'll have regulars now?" Brooke asked, tucking the donation money into a glittery zippered pencil case.

"Well, the soccer team probably," Aly said. "Jenica invited us to watch them play sometime." She slid the elastic off Brooke's braid.

"Ooh, that would be fun," Brooke said, scooting closer so Aly could brush her hair out. "I hope they won today."

"They're really good. I bet they did," Aly said, reaching for the hairbrush that was on her bed. "But really, I bet they could win without our sparkles."

"Maybe 'sparkle' should be in the name of our salon," Brooke said, squirming. "Ouch, Aly. I think I have a knot over there."

"Sorry," Aly said, putting the brush down and working on the knot with her fingers.

"How about Power to the Sparkle?" Brooke suggested.

"That sounds like a nail polish color," Aly said, "not like a salon."

"The Sparkle Sisters' Salon?" Brooke asked. Then she shook her head a little, but not enough to mess up Aly's unknotting. "That's not right either."

"How about . . . how about . . . Sparkle Spa."

Sparkle Spa. Sparkle Spa. Actually, it sounded perfect. Just like she'd done by choosing Lemon Aid for Heather's nails and suggesting two-person polishing during busy times, Brooke had the right idea at the right time.

"I love it!" Aly said.

Brooke twisted around and gave Aly a huge hug. The grand opening had been a grand success. And with a name like Sparkle Spa, Aly hoped things would only get better.

The Tanner sisters were smart. And strong. And sparkly. And their spa was too.

How to Give Yourself (or a Friend!) a Rainbow Pedicure

By Aly (and Brooke!)

＊ . ＊ ＊ . ＊ ＊ . ＊ ＊ . ＊ ＊ . ＊

What you need:

Paper towels

Polish remover

Cotton balls

Clear polish

Red polish

Orange polish

Yellow polish

Purple polish

Pink polish

What you do:

1. Put some paper towels on the floor so you don't have to worry about spilling polish. (Once, Aly spilled while she was painting my toes, and Mom got so, so mad and we still have a purple splotch on our carpet!)

2. Take one cotton ball and put some polish remover on it. If you have polish on your toes already, use enough to get it off. If you don't, just rub the remover over your nails to get off any dirt that might be on there. (Even if you can't see it very well, there still might be dirt!)

3. Rip off two paper towels. Twist the first one into a long tube and weave it back and forth between your toes to separate them a little bit more. Then do the same thing with the second paper towel for your other foot. You might need to tuck it in around your pinkie toe if it pops up and gets in your way while you polish.

4. Open up your clear polish and do a coat of clear on each nail. Then close the clear bottle up tight. (Aly usually starts with my big toes and works her way to my pinkies. You might want to do that too.)

5. Open up the red polish. Do a coat on each big toe. (When you're finished with each color, be sure to close the bottle up tight.) Open up the orange polish. Do a coat on each pointer toe. Open up the yellow polish. Do a coat on each middle toe. Open up the purple polish. Do a coat on each ring toe. Open up the pink polish. Do a coat on each pinkie toe.

6. Fan your toes a little to dry them a tiny bit, and then repeat step five. (This is when your colors start to look very bright—and sparkly if you have sparkle polish!)

7. Fan your toes a little again, and then open your clear polish. Do a top coat of clear polish on all your toes. Be sure to close the bottle up tight. (You can go in the same order you did last time!)

8. Now your toes have to dry. You can fan them for a long time, or sit and make a bracelet or read a book or watch TV or talk to your friend. Usually it takes about twenty minutes, but it could take longer. (After twenty minutes, you should check the polish really carefully by touching your big toe super lightly with your thumb. If it still feels sticky, keep waiting so you don't have to redo any nails!)

And now you should have a beautiful pedicure! Even after the polish is dry, you probably shouldn't wear socks and sneaker-type shoes for a while. Bare feet or sandals are better so all your hard work doesn't get smooshed. (And besides, then you can show people how fancy your toes look!)

Happy polishing!